Wherever We Go!

Story by Chani Altein
Artwork by Marc Lumer and Jovani Olivares

Hachai
PUBLISHING

You know, my friend Tzvi, when we're out for the day,
I always have fun and learn things on the way!

בס"ד
לד' הארץ ומלואה

This book belongs to:
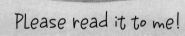

Please read it to me!

Glossary

Bracha: Blessing
Hashem: G-d
Kiddush Hashem: Sanctification of G-d's name
Mentsch: Proper human being

Wherever We Go!

Dedicated with love to my dear parents-in-law, Rabbi Leibel and Chavi Altein. C.A

To my dear parents, Gunter (Benjamin) and Linda (Esther) Lumer ע"ה
and my son Benny, who always keeps me on my toes! M.L.

Para mi mama, Juana Becerra, por todo su sacrificio. J.O.

First Edition – 5774 / 2014
Copyright © 2014 by HACHAI PUBLISHING
ALL RIGHTS RESERVED

Editor: D.L. Rosenfeld

Managing Editor: Yossi Leverton

 Layout: MarcLumerDesign.com

ISBN: 978-1-929628-79-7
LCCN: 2014942800

HACHAI PUBLISHING
Brooklyn, New York
Tel: 718-633-0100 • Fax: 718-633-0103

That's great, Little Benny, I love taking you
To the park, the museum, the farm or the zoo.
But to make Hashem happy, guess what I do –

I act like a mentsch, and I hope you will, too.

So if we are both at the park one fine day,
Enjoying an icy cold pop while we play,
We won't toss our trash in the air and not care,

But go find a trash can and stash it in there!

And if at the zoo, while walking around,
We spot a giraffe that's not making a sound,
We won't scream or shout and give him a fright,
But quietly point at that beautiful sight.

If one day we visit a farm for a treat
And pick lots of apples so fresh and so sweet

Let's make a nice bracha and be so polite,
Not gobble our apples in one giant bite!

And if at the fair, we happen to ride
A bright kiddie train on tracks round and wide,

We won't just run off and ignore everyone,
But first thank the driver for all of the fun!

If at the museum, one fine afternoon,
We're there to see rockets that went to the moon,
We won't push the kids in the line up ahead,

But stand and wait nicely for our turn instead!

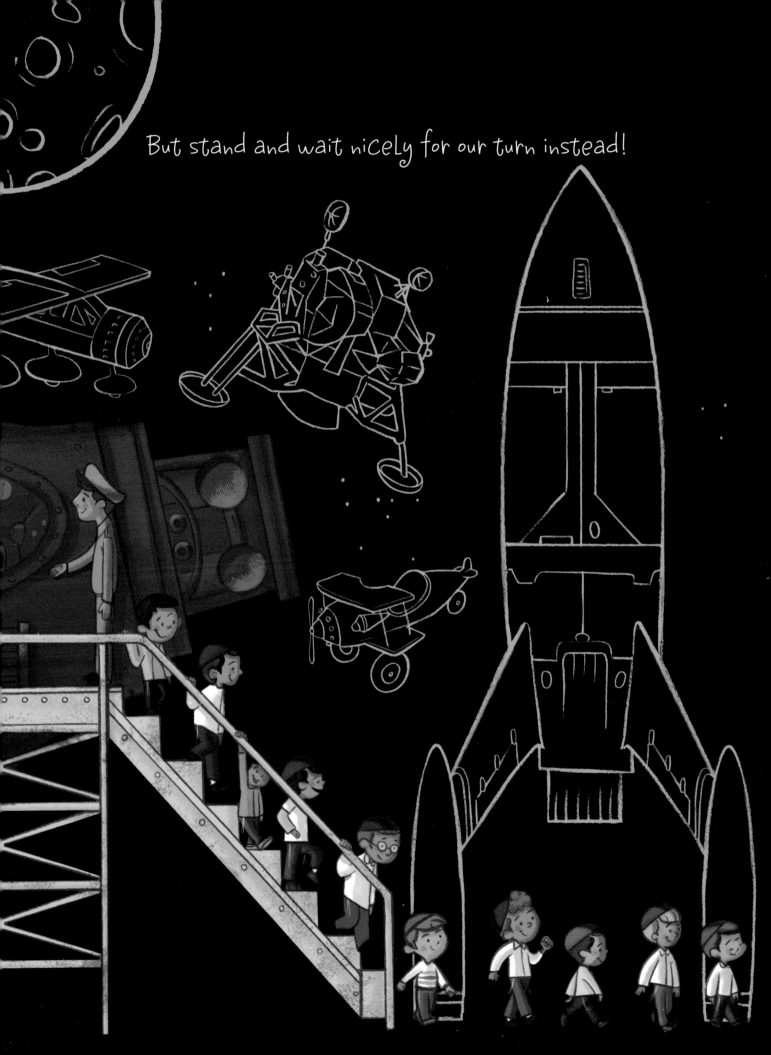

And if at the circus, we're happy to see
A clown who is giving balloons out for free,

We won't take them all, or pick two or three,
But choose only one, which is how it should be.

Now I see what you mean, now I know what you know,

I can make Hashem happy wherever I go!

So if at the toy store, where we always shop,
I see a boy's wallet he happened to drop,
I won't walk away as he loses his cash,

Instead, I'll return it to him in a flash.

And if at a playground, I suddenly spy
A kid tumble onto the ground with a cry,

I won't walk away, instead I will stay
To wait and make sure everything is okay.

Whenever we act in this wonderful way,
Here's what I think everybody will say,

"How lovely, how pleasant,

How nice and polite,

How helpful, how thoughtful,
How kind and how right.

What those kids are doing is something to see!

They follow Hashem; how great He must be!"

When we treat people well and act nicely to them,

We make what is called, "a Kiddush Hashem."